To my mum, who still calls me Mouse

First published in 2020 by Child's Play (International) Ltd
Ashworth Road, Bridgemead, Swindon SN5 7YD, UK

First published in USA in 2020 by Child's Play Inc
250 Minot Avenue, Auburn, Maine 04210

Distributed in Australia by Child's Play Australia Pty Ltd
Unit 10/20 Narabang Way, Belrose, Sydney, NSW 2085

ISBN 978-1-78628-463-1
CLP050919CPL11194631

Printed in Shenzhen, China

1 3 5 7 9 10 8 6 4 2

A catalogue record of this book
is available from the British Library

www.childs-play.com

I'm NOT a MOUSE!

Evgenia Golubeva

I love my mum, but for some reason she always calls me...

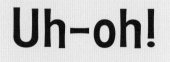

WHOOSH!

I don't like being called Mouse.
It's not fun getting changed
into a mouse at all...

There was the time I was about to blow out my birthday candles when Mum shouted...

Mouse!

And on the weekend I was playing in a football match when Mum cheered...

Go Mouse!

Another time I was roller-skating with Mum when...

Mouse!

And worst of all, I was petting
our cat when Mum came in...

Mouse!

I'd had enough!

So one day after school I had an idea!

I didn't answer when Mum called 'Mouse'. I kept quiet and didn't move.

She called me by my name and I liked that!

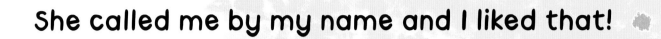

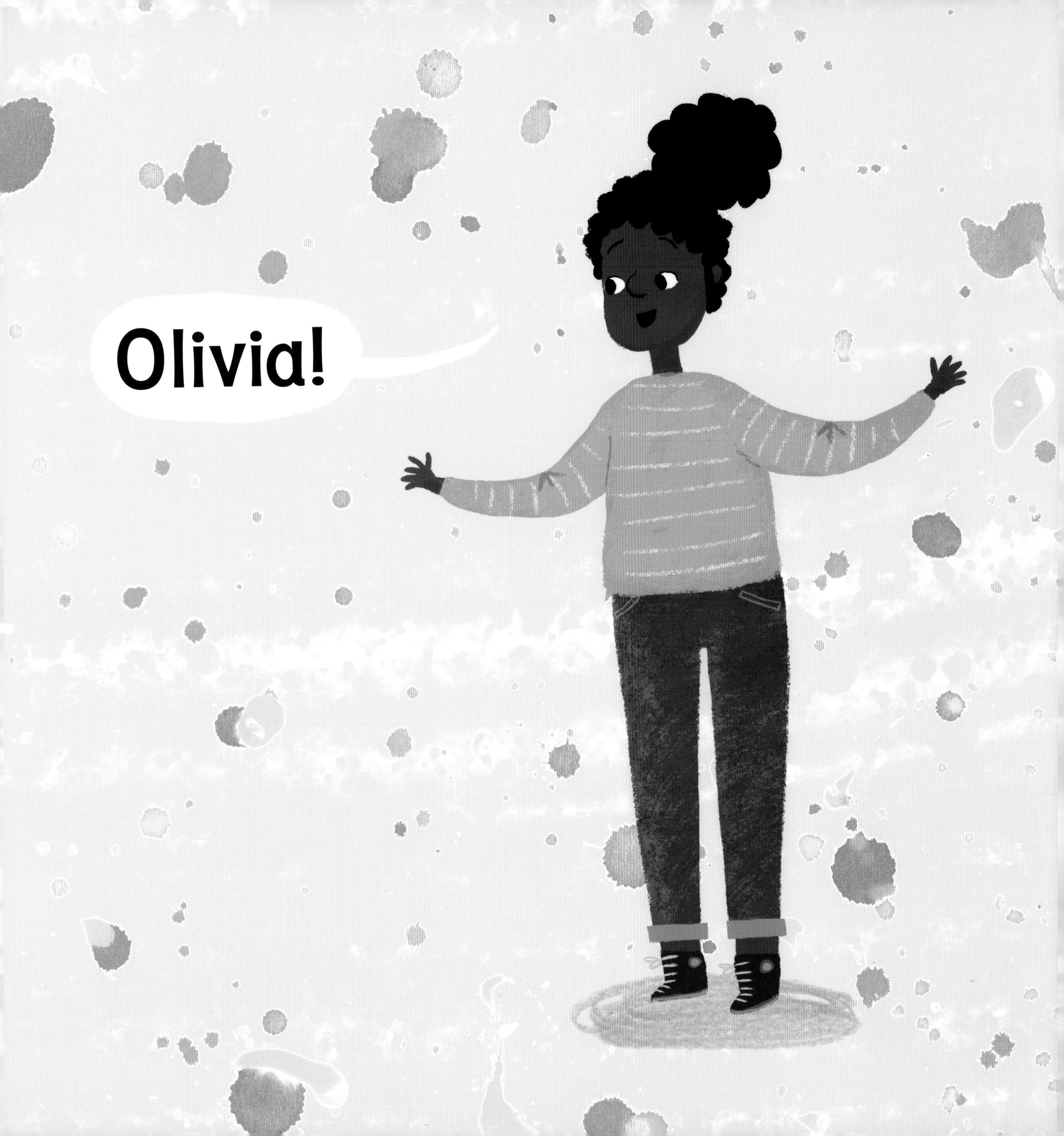
Olivia!

"I love you Olivia," said Mum.
"And I'm sorry. I only use your pet name because I love you very much."

But guess what happened then?!

My Little Pumpkin!

It was Lyla's dad
who had come to get her.

Then Husam's aunty arrived.

And when we went to the park
I couldn't believe my eyes!

Honey!

Our
Treasure!

My
Flower

Best of all, we went to the movies that evening
with Grandad and he said to Mum...

My Little Chicken!

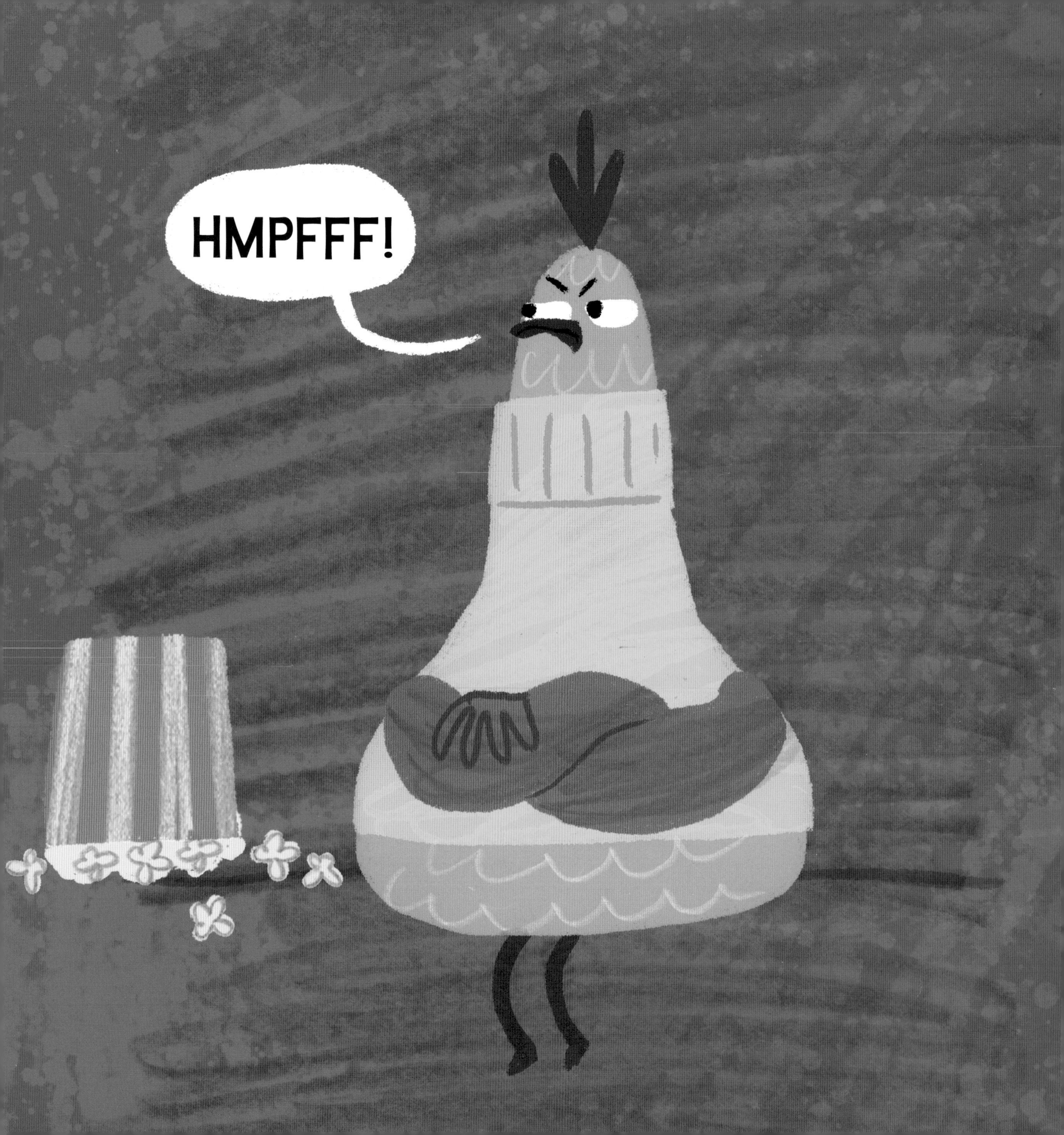
HMPFFF!